AMOS
GETS
MARRIED

YEARLING BOOKS/YOUNG YEARLINGS/YEARLING CLASSICS are designed especially to entertain and enlighten young people. Patricia Reilly Giff, consultant to this series, received her bachelor's degree from Marymount College and a master's degree in history from St. John's University. She holds a Professional Diploma in Reading and a Doctorate of Humane Letters from Hofstra University. She was a teacher and reading consultant for many years, and is the author of numerous books for young readers.

Gary Paulsen

AMOS GETS MARRIED

A YEARLING BOOK

Published by
Bantam Doubleday Dell Books for Young Readers
a division of
Bantam Doubleday Dell Publishing Group, Inc.
1540 Broadway
New York, New York 10036

ISBN: 0-440-40933-0

Printed in the United States of America

March 1995

10 9 8 7 6 5 4 3 2 1

OPM

AMOS GETS MARRIED

Chapter · 1

Duncan—Dunc—Culpepper sat on the ground in his front yard with his back against the porch. He was watching his best friend for life, Amos Binder, pace up and down the sidewalk.

"The school nurse said Melissa would be okay, Amos."

"I know what she said, but did you see the size of that goose egg on her forehead?"

"It'll go down. How did it happen, any-way?"

Amos stopped pacing and dropped to the ground beside him. "I was on my way to science class. Mrs. Leach said we were going to be dissecting earthworms, and I was think-

1

ing about all those poor little worms that were about to lose their lives."

"What do earthworms have to do with you knocking down Melissa Hansen?"

"Don't you ever wonder about some of the defenseless creatures we slice up in science lab? You know, like does it hurt and stuff?"

"Amos."

"Some of those worms could have families. We could be chopping up someone's mother or grandmother, or—"

"Amos! What happened to Melissa?"

"Like I said. I was thinking about the worms when I heard the pay phone ring outside the nurse's office."

"So?"

"So I figured since Melissa knows I have to pass the nurse's office on my way to science class, she was calling to talk to me. She probably wanted to see how my day was going and talk about the worms and things like that."

Dunc nodded. He knew Amos was crazy in love with Melissa Hansen and that he had this strange idea she might actually call him someday. She had never called him in her entire life and gave no indication that she ever would. In fact, Melissa gave no indication that she knew Amos existed as a life-form. But that didn't stop Amos from hoping.

"Anyway," Amos continued, "I was in a real hurry to get to the phone, on account of she likes me to get it on that all-important first ring and everything. So I crawled up on Jerk Jergin's back and yelled for everybody to make way. I knew they would move because Jerk's a pretty good-sized kid."

Dunc nodded again. "He should be. He's been in the same grade for the last six years. I heard a rumor that he has a wife, two kids, and an after-school job at the steel mill."

"That's why I chose him," Amos said. "But it didn't quite work the way I planned."

"What happened?"

"I think I must have caught Jerk a little off guard. He pulled me up over the top of his head and wadded me up into a ball. Then he sort of punted me to the end of the hall. That's when I hit Melissa. It wasn't her on the phone after all." Amos stood up and started pacing again. "It was awful. I slammed her face into a bank of lockers. She'll probably never forgive me."

"Try not to worry, Amos. The nurse said Melissa was unconscious for a few minutes and doesn't remember anything that happened."

"Somebody is bound to tell her, and then she'll probably want to cancel our date."

"Amos, you know you don't have a date with Melissa."

"I don't yet. But I was planning on asking her to the Winter Harvest Dance."

"Amos, it's spring. Early spring. The Winter Harvest Dance isn't until next year."

"I know, but I wanted to give her plenty of time to think about it."

Dunc stood and stretched. "I better get started on my homework." He picked up the newspaper on his way into the house.

Amos followed him. The screen door banged shut behind him. "You can't do homework now! I'm having a crisis!"

Dunc headed for the kitchen. "I'm having a peanut butter and jelly."

"How can you eat or do homework at a time like this?"

Dunc carefully wiped the peanut butter off the knife, rinsed it, and put it away. "The way I see it, you really don't have a problem."

Amos stared at him. "No problem? Melissa may never speak to me again."

"That's what I mean. She's never spoken to you before, so you haven't lost anything."

Amos sighed. "Maybe I should go over and apologize."

Dunc shook his head. "She's probably resting. And besides, there's still a chance she doesn't know it was you. If I were you, I'd wait until social studies class tomorrow and see if she acts different or anything."

"I don't know . . ."

"Trust me."

"You *had* to say that. Every time you say that, something goes wrong."

Dunc ignored him. "Are you doing your homework over here?"

"I don't have any homework."

"What about the essay Mrs. Wormwood gave us on the family? We're supposed to do five pages."

Amos waved his hand. "Oh, that. I'll do it during passing period tomorrow."

"You can't do a five-page paper in five minutes—while you're walking."

"Why not?"

Dunc sighed. "Come on. I'll help you write your paper."

"I was hoping you'd say that."

Chapter · 2

"Where's your homework?" Dunc pedaled his bike close to Amos so he could hear.

"It's in my back pocket."

"You put a five-page report in your back pocket?"

Amos nodded. "It was a tight fit, but I kept folding and stuffing until it all went in." He stood on the pedals to show Dunc the bulge in his back pocket.

"Did it ever occur to you that you might get a better grade if your report wasn't all crumpled up?"

Amos shook his head. "You don't understand teachers. You have to try and think like them. If you were a teacher and you came to a paper with no wrinkles, in perfect condition, with my name on it, what would you think?"

"That someone else did it."

"Bingo!"

Dunc coasted for a few feet. "Still, you should make an effort . . ."

Amos wasn't listening. They were passing Melissa's house. He always rode by slowly in hopes that he might catch a glimpse of her.

They were almost to the end of the block when he saw her. She was standing at the window. Her long golden hair was blowing in the wind.

"Look, Dunc! There she is."

"Watch where you're going, Amos! You nearly ran into me."

"Isn't she beautiful?"

"I guess. If you don't count that ugly purple bruise and the bandage on her forehead." Dunc pedaled up ahead. "We're going to be late for school if you don't come on."

Amos was about to turn and follow, when the most unthinkable thing in the whole world happened.

Melissa looked down from the window—and waved.

Amos was stunned. He stared until he lost control of his bike and rammed a fire hydrant. When Dunc came back for him, Amos was on the ground wearing the front wheel of his bicycle around his neck.

"Are you okay?"

"She loves me!"

Dunc pulled the wheel off of Amos's head and put it back on the front of the bike. He stood on the frame and tried to straighten it. "I don't know if you can ride it. You may have to push it to school." He looked at Amos. "Can you walk?"

"Walk? I can fly! Melissa waved at me."

Dunc glanced at Melissa's house. He didn't see anyone. He looked back at Amos, who was sitting on the ground with an absurd grin on his face. "You're imagining things again."

"No, really." Amos pointed at the house. "She stood at that window, looked right at me, and waved."

Dunc studied the window. The curtains were flapping in the breeze. "I'm sure it was

9

an optical illusion. Come on, we're going to miss first period."

Amos stood and took one last look at the house. He squeezed his eyes shut and then opened them. No one was at the window. "It seemed real. I saw her dimples and everything."

Amos threw his leg over his bike and tried to pedal. Only one pedal worked, the front tire flopped as it went around, and from the back, his bike looked like it was traveling sideways.

Dunc rode more slowly so Amos could keep up. "It's funny how the mind can play tricks on you. I read a book once where this guy went without eating for two weeks, and he thought he saw George Washington crossing the Delaware."

Amos frowned. "But it seemed so real! She looked right at me."

"Optical illusions always seem real. People in the desert who are dying of thirst sometimes think they see water and actually start swimming in the sand." Dunc looked back at him. "I wouldn't worry about it. It happens all the time."

"If you say so . . ."

A station wagon pulled up beside them and stopped at the stop sign. Melissa's mother was driving her to school. Melissa looked out the passenger window. She saw Amos—and smiled.

Amos's eyes popped wide open. He stared at the car instead of watching where he was going. He ran through the Swansons' white picket fence and landed head-first in their rose bushes.

When Dunc heard the crash, he turned around and rode back to his friend. "You definitely have a problem."

"But she"—Amos sputtered—"you didn't see. She . . . I saw her. . . ."

Dunc helped him up. "It's okay, Amos. I'll talk to your parents. We'll get you some professional help."

Chapter · 3

"Are you sure you don't want to go home? You look a little pale." Dunc helped Amos lock what was left of his bike to the bike rack.

Amos headed toward the school in a daze. "Melissa . . . car . . . smile . . ."

Dunc led him through the double doors and down the hall. "Here's your class, Amos. Do you think you'll be all right?"

Amos walked into his math class muttering, "Waved . . . me . . . love . . . Melissa."

By lunchtime, Dunc thought Amos seemed a little better. He still wasn't quite back to normal, but he was able to speak in semi-intelligent sentences.

Dunc pushed him through the cafeteria line. He took Amos's elbow and led him to a table. When they were seated, Dunc reached into his book bag, took out a thick book, and plopped it on the table.

"Do you see this, Amos? This book is going to help us get to the root of your problem." He watched Amos dip a piece of lettuce in his chocolate milk.

Dunc winced and took a deep breath. "This is a book on psychiatric abnormalities. Chapter fourteen describes you perfectly. It says when a person thinks about another person to the point of shutting out everything else, he may begin to imagine that he actually has a relationship with that person. Are you following me so far?"

Amos nodded and dipped another piece of lettuce. "Melissa loves me."

"No, Amos. That's what I'm talking about. She doesn't love you. It says right here in the book—you imagined the whole thing, and you made your mind believe it was real."

Amos squinted at the book and scratched his head. "I don't think that's the way it happened."

"The book says there are several methods of treatment we can try. I personally think we should go with the electric shock therapy. That's the one where we run electric currents through your brain over and over until you're all better."

Amos looked at him. "And you think *I'm* crazy?"

"I had a feeling you wouldn't like that one." Dunc ran his finger down the page. "How about 'deprogramming'?"

"Does it have anything to do with electricity?"

"No. What you do on this one is tell yourself out loud over and over that what you think happened—didn't happen."

"But Dunc, I saw her . . ."

"You *thought* you saw her. But in reality you only saw what your mind wanted you to see." Dunc patted the book. "It's all right here on page three hundred and seven."

Amos looked confused. "If you say so."

"Let's try it. Tell yourself it didn't happen."

"It didn't happen. But Dunc—"

"No buts. If you want it to work, you have to keep saying it until you've put the

15

whole thing out of your mind, and then you'll be cured."

Amos started. "It didn't happen. It didn't happen. . . ."

Dunc kept a tally on the back of a napkin. "You're doing great, Amos. You're up to a hundred fifty-seven. Is it out of your system yet?"

"I don't know."

"We want to be sure. Keep going until the bell rings."

Chapter·4

"I feel a lot better." Amos followed Dunc down the hall. "I should be fine now."

"That's good, because Melissa is in our next class—social studies. Now remember, if your mind starts playing tricks on you, just tell yourself it didn't happen, and it will go away."

The boys sat down in the back of the classroom just as the bell rang. Dunc took out his social studies homework. Amos checked his back pocket but couldn't find his. It had worked its way out somewhere between gym class and the cafeteria.

Mrs. Wormwood was writing on the board when the door opened and Melissa walked in. The teacher turned. "Young lady, you're late."

Melissa flashed one of her most angelic smiles. "I'm sorry, Mrs. Wormwood. I was doing an errand for the principal."

Mrs. Wormwood patted her on the head. "I was sure an honor student like yourself wouldn't be late without a good reason. Sit down, dear."

Melissa moved to her desk. But before she sat down, she turned to Amos—and winked.

Amos dropped his head on his desk and closed his eyes. "It's not real. It didn't happen. It's not real. . . ."

Mrs. Wormwood cleared her throat. "Now, class. Today we will begin working on a special project dealing with living skills. You will each choose a partner . . ."

Dunc looked over at Amos. Amos was hitting his head against his desk and mumbling under his breath.

". . . of the opposite sex, who will be your pretend husband or wife for the next week. We will conduct a mock marriage ceremony. You and your partner will set up a budget for rent, groceries, bills, and other

18

expenses. Your grade will depend on how well you work together with your partner, how realistic your budget is, and, of course, how well it balances. Any questions?"

Herman Snodgrass wiped his nose with the back of his sleeve and raised his hand.

"Yes, Herman?"

"Do we have to do it?"

Mrs. Wormwood gave him *the look*. "No, Herman. Not if you would rather flunk my class and have me for your teacher again next year."

Herman slid down in his seat and stuck out his bottom lip. "No way."

A group of girls in the front row giggled.

Mrs. Wormwood slapped her desk with a yardstick. "Order. I want order." The yard-stick broke and the whole class burst out laughing.

Dunc used the opportunity to whisper to Amos, "Are you okay?"

"It didn't happen. . . . I only imagined it. . . . It never really happened."

Mrs. Wormwood finally gained control of the class. "Since there are fewer girls than boys in our class, we will begin our project by letting the girls choose the partner they would like to work with. When I call your name, please stand and tell me the name of the partner you have chosen."

"Bertha Abercromby?"

Amos opened one eye and looked up at Tall Bertha. She stood beside her desk with her finger in her mouth and glanced around the room. For one awful moment her eyes rested on him, but then she looked away. He let out a deep sigh of relief.

Bertha grinned. She took her finger out of her mouth and pointed at the back of the room. "I choose him—Duncan Culpepper."

Dunc's shoulder's drooped. He slumped down in his desk. His worst nightmare had come true. It wasn't so bad that Bertha was almost two feet taller than he was and outweighed him by thirty pounds. That didn't bother him nearly as much as the fact that Bertha was a mess. She was the most unorganized person Dunc knew—except for Amos, of course.

Amos listened with his fingers crossed as Mrs. Wormwood continued down the list. About half the boys had been chosen. Amos was still in the clear. Maybe by some miracle he wouldn't be chosen.

The teacher finally reached the end of the list of girls. No one had picked him. Mrs. Wormwood started to close her book, when something caught her eye. "Oh dear, it seems I've overlooked someone." She paused. "Melissa Hansen?"

Melissa slowly stood beside her desk. She looked from Donny Wilson to Jimmy Johnson. She batted her long lashes and smiled at the teacher.

"I choose . . . Amos—*the Hunk*—Binder."

Dunc's mouth fell open. He looked over at Amos. The desk was empty.

Amos had fallen into the aisle on the floor, out cold.

Chapter · 5

Amos was in Dunc's room looking in the mirror above the dresser. First he studied his left profile and then his right. "I never really thought of myself as a hunk before."

"Neither has anyone else in their right mind." Dunc was at his desk working out a foolproof budget so that every penny would be accounted for in his report to Mrs. Wormwood. "There. I think I have our first month ready. The debit column is zero and all possible expenses have been met. I think we definitely have an A-plus paper here."

Amos sprawled across Dunc's bed. "Don't you think you better ask your wife what she thinks about it? After all, it's her grade too."

"Ugh!" Dunc shuddered. "Don't remind me. I'd like to forget all about that part of the assignment."

Amos smiled dreamily. "I'm meeting my little cupcake at the mall later. We're going to go pretend shopping. You should come with us. It would give you an idea of what kind of stuff girls like to spend money on."

"I don't care what kind of stuff girls spend money on. And another thing, Bertha Abercromby is not my wife—will never be my wife—in this or any other lifetime. If this thing were real, I'd already have filed for divorce."

"Bertha told Melissa that she really likes you."

Dunc made a face. "She doesn't even turn in her homework."

"So?" Amos said. "I lose my homework all the time and you still like me."

"That's different."

Amos sat up. "Your problem is, you just don't understand women."

Dunc looked at him. "I think you're losing it again. Since when have you become an expert on females?"

Amos shrugged. "I must be doing something right. Melissa picked me, didn't she?"

"I've been meaning to talk to you about that."

Amos held up his hand. "Don't try to tell me my mind is playing tricks on me. This time I have witnesses."

"No, I know she picked you all right. But the question is—why?"

Amos threw his chest out. "Because I'm a hunk."

"Melissa Hansen never even knew you were alive until today. Don't you think that's a little strange?"

"No. It was bound to happen sooner or later. She finally came to her senses and realized we're meant for each other."

"I have a theory about that. I think that bump on the head you gave her is causing her to act weird. You know, do things she wouldn't normally do."

"Thanks a lot."

"I'm serious, Amos. Sometimes people who get hit on the head act strange for a while."

"Are you saying that Melissa doesn't love me—that she's just lost her marbles?"

"Something like that."

Amos thought about it for a few minutes. "You mean she could come back to her old self at any time?"

Dunc nodded. "It's a possibility."

Amos hunched forward. "This is terrible. Melissa doesn't really love me, but she doesn't know she doesn't really love me."

"Don't worry, Amos. Sometimes these head injury things last for a long time. Sometimes months or even years."

Amos's face brightened. "Really?"

"Yeah. I read in that psychology book about this guy who went for seven years before he figured out he was messed up."

"What happened to him?"

"When he finally came to his senses, it was too much for him and he jumped in front of a train."

Amos sagged. "Great. Melissa will be madly in love with me until she wakes up, and then she'll go out and jump off a cliff."

26

Chapter · 6

"Did you hear that strange announcement yesterday?" Dunc changed gears and coasted his bike down a hill.

Amos passed him. "Yeah. It came over the intercom during math class. The principal said for everybody to make sure they locked their lockers because some fruitcake is ripping off school supplies. Now, that's what I call sick. If I was a thief, I could find better stuff to take than school supplies."

"I've been making a list of possible suspects. It would have to be someone who could move up and down the halls without anyone thinking anything about it. I've narrowed it down to school employees."

"You mean like the principal or one of the teachers?"

"Maybe."

"Do you have anyone in particular in mind?"

"Not yet. I was going to work on it today."

"I'm glad you decided to come with me to the mall instead." Amos stood up on the pedals of his bike and powered up a small hill. Dunc had helped him hammer out the dents and although the wheels still squeaked, it seemed to work okay. "Since we don't know when Melissa may snap out of this head injury thing, it might be good for both of us to be there."

Dunc jumped the curb and neatly swerved to avoid the Seaversons' dalmatian. "I'm only going along for scientific reasons. I want to record Melissa's actions for future analysis. And don't forget, you promised to help me with the case later."

"Are you sure you're not going because deep down you really want to go shopping with Bertha Abercromby?"

Dunc stopped. Dead.

Amos pedaled on for a few yards before

he noticed Dunc wasn't coming. He stopped to look back. "What's the matter?"

"You didn't tell me Tall Bertha would be there."

Amos dug the toe of his tennis shoe into the ground. "I didn't? I thought for sure I'd mentioned it."

Dunc turned his bike around.

"Where are you going?" Amos asked.

"Home. You can fill me in on all the strange things Melissa does later."

"But Dunc, I promised Melissa we'd be there. She and Bertha are probably waiting on us right now."

Dunc pushed off. " 'Bye."

Amos pedaled up beside him. "You have to come with me. This may be the most important day of my life! Besides, you promised you'd come if I helped you find clues later."

Dunc pedaled faster.

Amos was having a hard time keeping up with him. "I hate to bring this up, but—"

"There's absolutely nothing you can say that will get me to walk around the mall, in front of people, with Bertha Abercromby."

"Grades."

"What?"

"Mrs. Wormwood said in order to get the best grade, we had to go shopping with our partners at least one time. This could be your time. Then it would be over, and you'd never have to see Bertha again. Except at school."

Dunc stopped again. His lip curled, and he wrinkled his nose. "I don't know how teachers get away with some of this stuff. I'm fairly sure it's unconstitutional. And if it isn't, it ought to be."

"Are you coming?"

"I guess so. But"—Dunc held up one finger—"I don't want to stay too long. It might give people the wrong idea."

It was late afternoon, and the bike rack at the Pioneer Mall was jammed because the video arcade had just put in a new game, Invasion of the Sewer Dwellers.

"I see the girls." Amos waved toward some tables in the Ice Cream Heaven. "Do I look all right?"

Dunc looked him up and down. "You look the same as always."

"Is that good?"

"In Melissa's condition, I don't think it matters."

Amos was about to ask what that was supposed to mean when Melissa walked up to them with Bertha trailing close behind. She took Amos's arm. "Hello, sweety-kins. I thought you'd never get here."

Amos turned red from head to toe. He looked over his shoulder and whispered to Dunc, "I hope she *never* wakes up."

Bertha chewed on her bottom lip. "Hello, Duncan."

Dunc looked at her shoes. They were untied and she had on two different colors of socks. He cleared his throat. "Uh, we better get on with this shopping stuff. I've got important things to do."

Melissa led Amos down the mall. "I think we should go to the jewelry store first." She winked at Amos. "You know, to check out the cost of wedding rings."

Amos grinned from ear to ear. "Whatever you say, dear."

Dunc followed the three of them around the mall looking at shoes, sweaters, and hair bows until he couldn't take it anymore.

31

"I think I better call it a day." He looked at Bertha. "I'll go home and adjust the budget to reflect some of the things we looked at. We shouldn't need to get together again. This ought to wrap it up."

Melissa looked at Amos with big innocent blue eyes. "You're not leaving too, are you?"

"Uh, well . . ."

"I was hoping you would show me how to play that new arcade game, and then maybe later you could, you know, walk me home."

"Ye-es!"

Chapter·7

Amos followed Dunc to his locker. "It couldn't have been all that bad."

Dunc glared at him and slammed his locker door. "Because of you staying at the mall with Melissa, I was forced to walk Tall Bertha home in front of the entire world, and you don't think it was all that bad? Herman Snodgrass drew a heart with our names in it on the chalk board in gym class. Now Bertha is giving me the googly eye and calling me at home every five minutes. I have to pay my sister ten cents a call to hang up on her."

"It's mostly your own fault," Amos said.

"*My* fault?"

"You're the one who told me this deal with Melissa might not last. I have to take advantage of every minute."

"Even if it means embarrassing your best friend?"

"I said I was sorry. I'll make it up to you. I'll even stay after today and help you work on this school thief thing. You name it, I'll do it."

Dunc rubbed his chin. "We-ll . . ."

Amos took a step backward. "I'm not sure I like the look in your eye."

"It just so happens that I do have something you can help me with. Since the school is short one custodian right now, I made arrangements with the principal for us to help out. She thought it was nice of us to offer."

"*Us?*"

"It'll be a great cover."

Amos leaned against the wall. "Why do I feel like I've been set up?"

"Come on. I have to get you in position."

"For what?"

"The principal said we could be ten minutes late to our afternoon classes for the rest of this week. But we have to look like

34

we're cleaning or something." Dunc led him to the custodians' closet. "Here, you take this broom. Act like you're sweeping the main hall. Watch for anything suspicious."

"Where are you going to be?"

"I'll be back and forth between the other hall and the gym."

The bell rang, and Amos started pushing the broom down the hall. "The things I do in the name of friendship."

"What was that, sugar-lips?"

Amos turned and found Melissa. "Oh, it was nothing, lamb chop. Hey, aren't you going to be late for class?"

Melissa smiled. "I'm running another errand for the principal. See you after school—snookems."

Amos waved and watched her walk down the hall until she disappeared. He pushed the broom around dreamily until Dunc came for him.

"Did you see anything?" Dunc asked.

"No. How about you?"

Dunc shook his head. "Whoever it is, is bound to slip up sooner or later. We'll catch them. Come on, let's get this stuff back to the supply closet."

Amos stepped inside the closet and reached to hook his broom on one of the clips. He accidentally bumped the shelf above with the broom handle, and a can of cleanser fell off. Amos and the room were covered with blue powder.

Dunc picked up the can. "Oh well, we'll have to clean it up later. Right now, we'd better go before we get in trouble." He climbed the stepladder to put the can back. He stopped and stared. "Amos, you've done it again."

"I know." Amos blinked, and some of the powder fell off his lashes onto his nose. "Aaa-choo!"

"Look at this." Dunc held up a stack of notebooks, some new pencils, and a book bag.

"Now, why would the custodian keep a bunch of school supplies up there where you can hardly reach them?" Amos asked.

"Don't you get it?" Dunc stepped down. "These are some of the stolen school supplies the principal was talking about. We've solved the case on our first try. Ralph the custodian must have done it."

"That's nice. You go turn him in, and I'll get cleaned up."

"We can't do that."

"Look, if I don't get this stuff off me, I'm going to sneeze my brains out." He sneezed again.

"I mean we can't turn Ralph in just yet."

"Why not?"

"Because he'll just deny it and say someone else put the stuff here. No, we have to catch him red-handed."

"Aaa-choo!" Amos wiped his nose on the dust rag. "You catch him red-handed. I need a shower before I die."

Amos backed out the door into a wall. Or what felt like a wall. It was a man with a deep voice.

"Who do you think you're going to catch red-handed?"

Chapter·8

"That was some fast talking you did today." Amos threw a dart at the dart board on Dunc's wall. "Telling Ralph you were going to use me as a human scrub brush for the boys' showers was a stroke of genius." He threw another dart and missed by a good five inches. The dart stuck in the wall.

Dunc cringed. "Would you mind trying a little harder to hit the board?"

Dunc had a thing about keeping his room in perfect condition. That included no unnecessary holes in the wall. Unlike Amos, who figured holes were okay as long as you didn't get in trouble over them. Like the time he tried out his uncle's flame thrower and burned a hole the size of a truck in his floor. His mom had to call the fire department, and his dad grounded him until he was ninety-nine or dead—whichever came first.

"Sure." Amos tried a shot behind his back. The dart stuck in the carpet. "How'd you think of that story, anyway?"

Dunc shrugged. "You sort of looked the part with that cleanser all over you, and I figured if Ralph thought we were saving him some work, he'd probably let us go."

"It worked. So what happens now?"

"Now we need a foolproof plan to catch Ralph in the act."

"And unless I miss my guess, you just happen to have one, right?"

Dunc nodded.

"And it involves me doing something totally stupid and making a fool out of myself, as usual, I suppose?"

"No. This one barely involves you at all."

"That's good, because I promised Melissa we'd go Rollerblading after school tomorrow."

"I didn't know you could Rollerblade."

"I can't. My sister Amy is going to teach me later today."

"That was nice of her."

"Nice? Amy doesn't know the meaning of the word. I had to promise her my allowance for six months, wash the dishes on her night, clean her room, and pretty much wait on her hand and foot for the rest of my life."

"That seems like a lot. Do you think learning to Rollerblade is worth it?"

A dreamy look came over Amos. "For Melissa, I'd swim an ocean full of sharks, climb the highest mountain, walk on hot coals, cross a—"

"I get the picture." Dunc took a note pad off his desk. "We need to make a list of everything in your locker."

Amos blinked. "My locker?"

"Yeah. We need to make a list so that when Ralph takes something, we'll know what it was."

"Out of all the lockers in school, what makes you think Ralph is going to choose my locker?"

"Because you're going to leave it open."

"Uh-uh. I never leave my locker open.

41

Not since that time Jimmy Farrell put Mrs. Leach's ferret in there and it tried to eat the left half of my body."

"This time you're going to leave it open on purpose so Ralph will take some of your stuff and we can catch him in the act."

Amos started to throw another dart. He stopped. "Wait a minute—why does it have to be my locker?"

"I thought about using my locker, but it's not messy enough. A good thief would figure that I would be able to spot something missing right away. You, on the other hand, might not notice something missing from your locker, well—ever." Dunc made columns on the note pad. "Okay. Try as hard as you can to remember everything in your locker."

Amos thought about it. "My notebook is in there. My gym clothes, math book, a banana peel, pencils, worms, English book, a few old—"

"Hold it." Dunc quit writing and studied him. "Worms?"

Amos looked at the floor.

Dunc moved closer. "Worms?"

Amos shifted. "I sort of borrowed the earthworms from the science lab."

"Amos, you can't go around taking things from the science lab. That's—that's stealing."

"I told you. I didn't steal them—I borrowed them. I thought later I would kind of let them run free."

Dunc raised one eyebrow. "Worms? Run free?"

"Hey," Amos said, "I'm saving lives here."

"I hope you know what you're doing." Dunc looked down at the note pad. "All right, where were we? Do you have anything else in your locker?"

"Let's see. There's a sweatshirt with one sleeve missing—from the ferret incident—about two pounds of trash, my science book, a half-finished report on the external anatomy of a short-horned grasshopper, and a couple of soda cans I was saving to recycle later."

Dunc catalogued each item. "Is that it?"

"That's everything since Christmas vacation. Before that, I'm not sure."

Dunc moved to his desk and picked up a clear plastic bag with light pink powder in it. He held it up. "This is going to help us make sure Ralph doesn't get away."

"What is it?"

"It's invisible ink powder. I learned how to make it from my latest issue of *Junior Scientist*. We'll sprinkle it on all the stuff in your locker, and a few minutes after Ralph touches it, the ends of his fingers will be smeared with black ink. It doesn't wash off. It has to wear off. That way, even if he denies taking the things in your locker, we'll still have the proof we need to turn him in."

Chapter·9

"Get your foot out of my face."

"Hold still, Amos. I can't see anything when you move around like that."

"Why don't we trade places? I'll stand on your shoulders and look through the vent in the door. Better yet, let's get out of this closet and watch from someplace that doesn't smell like something was buried in it recently."

"Shh. There he is!"

"Who?"

"Ralph the custodian. And he's almost to your locker."

"I hope he gets there soon. My shoulders are starting to go numb."

Dunc put his foot on Amos's head. "He's

looking around. He's standing right in front of it. Oh, no!"

"What happened? Did he take something?"

Dunc scrambled to the floor and opened the closet door a crack. "That's strange. He didn't seem to notice that your locker was open, and now he's leaving. Come on—let's follow him. He's probably going for a locker at the other end of the hall."

The boys tiptoed down the hall a few yards behind him. Ralph turned around twice. The first time, they ducked behind a garbage can. The second time, they weren't as lucky. Dunc grabbed Amos's shirt and pulled him into the nearest room.

The teachers' lounge.

Two of the teachers were at the coffee machine. Another one was running off photocopies, and a couple were sitting on the sofa eating doughnuts and discussing their night jobs. When they spotted the boys, the conversation stopped. Every teacher turned and stared.

Amos took a good look around. "So this is what it looks like. I always wondered what they did in here."

Dunc elbowed Amos in the ribs, then grabbed him, and made for the door. "Excuse us. Wrong room."

"You two hold it right there." Mr. Grossman, the gym teacher, barred the door. "What are you doing out of class? Don't you know that this is a restricted area?"

Dunc fumbled in his pocket for his pass from the principal. "Ms. Fishbeck gave us permission to be a few minutes late to class. We're the new custodians' helpers."

"Ooh, how nice." Mrs. Pittbottom stood up. "I think that's wonderful. You boys can start in here. This room never seems to get cleaned properly."

"Uh"—Dunc looked at his watch—"we'd love to clean in here, we really would. But we have to get to class right now. Come on, Amos. We better hurry."

They edged around Mr. Grossman and ran down the hall.

Dunc stopped running when they turned the corner. He was breathing hard. "Made it. Now let's see if we can spot Ralph before it's time for us to be in class."

"Wait until I see that Donny Wilson," Amos said.

"Why?"

"He said the teachers have hundreds of little shrunken heads and they keep them on this long string in the teachers' lounge. He said they belong to former students. And when they have teachers' meetings in there, they're really holding secret ceremonies to decide on their next victim. I didn't see one shrunken head in there. Did you?"

"Amos, I can't believe you'd pay attention to anything Donny Wilson says. He still claims Michael Jordan pulled up to his house in a white limousine and asked if he could come in and use the bathroom."

"That didn't happen either?"

"Amos."

"Well, it's possible."

Dunc held up his hand. "Here comes Ralph, and it looks like he's hiding something. Quick—act nonchalant."

"Non-what?"

"Casual. Act casual."

"Oh." Amos put his hands in his pockets and pretended to be reading the bulletin board. Ralph had something hidden behind his back. When he passed the boys, he moved it around to his front.

"We've got him now," Dunc whispered. "He went into that rest room. All we have to do is catch him with the goods."

"Wait. I'm not so sure about this. Maybe we should get reinforcements. After all, Ralph is a pretty big guy."

"Come on, Amos. It's now or never."

"I vote for never. What's a few notebooks and pencils, anyway?"

"Melissa."

"What does Melissa have to do with this? Ralph didn't take her notebook."

"If you were to solve this case, Melissa would be so impressed, she'd adore you."

Amos straightened his collar. "In case you haven't noticed, Melissa already adores me."

"Yeah, but that's because she got knocked in the head. I'm talking about permanent adoration, even after she comes back to her regular self."

"You mean you think she'll wake up, remember that I saved everybody's school supplies, and love me forever after all?"

"Something like that."

"Okay. But if I'm going to get the credit, let me do the talking."

Dunc followed him to the door of the rest room. Amos squared his shoulders and stuck his chin out. He put his hand on the door and pushed. "All right, Ralph. This is a citizen's arrest. We've caught you red-handed . . . smoking?"

Ralph quickly threw his cigarette in the toilet. "I'm sorry. I've been trying to quit. I know it's against school rules. Please, please—don't turn me in. I need this job."

Amos glared at Dunc. "One moment, Ralph. Let me confer with my assistant." Amos pushed Dunc up against the sink. "I thought you told me he was stealing school supplies. I didn't know we were busting him for breaking the school no-smoking policy."

"We're not busting him." Dunc looked under Amos's arm. "Sorry, Ralph. We've made a tiny mistake here. We'll just be on our way to class now. You, ah—you really should do something about that habit though. See ya."

The boys quietly backed out the door.

"I can't believe we just did that," Amos said. "We made a grown man cry."

Dunc looked at his watch. "I can't believe

we're twenty minutes late to class. Do you have your math book?"

"No. I was hoping Ralph would take it, and then I'd have an excuse not to bring it to class anymore."

"Hurry up and get it. I'll wait for you by the water fountain."

"Duunnc!"

"What is it, Amos? We don't have time to mess around."

"I think you better see this."

Dunc moved around the bank of lockers. Amos was standing in front of his. The door was hanging wide open.

The locker was empty.

Chapter · 10

"Do you mind if we stop by Melissa's house on the way home? She said she has a present for me."

"No." Dunc straightened his handlebars and concentrated on the road.

"Is something bothering you?"

"It's the case. I was *sure* Ralph was guilty. I guess someone else must have put that stuff in the custodians' closet. I don't have another suspect now that Ralph is out of the picture."

"I told you, we'll go to school early tomorrow and look for somebody with ink-stained fingertips. It'll be a cinch."

Dunc sighed. "I know. It's just that I was

so sure it was Ralph. How could I have been so wrong? I'm sorry about all your stuff."

"I'm not. Now I don't have to bring any books to school. I just hope whoever took the worms takes good care of them. I kind of started to like them. I named some of them and thought maybe I could train them to come, or heel . . ."

Amos pulled up in Melissa's driveway. Dunc stopped at the curb.

"Aren't you coming in?" Amos asked.

"No, I'll wait out here. You two are enough to make anybody throw up, with all those dumb names you call each other."

"Hi, honey-muffin!" Melissa waved at Amos from the upstairs window.

"See what I mean?" Dunc said.

Amos spread his arms out. "Can I help it? The girl's crazy about me. Be right back."

The front door opened, and Amos disappeared inside. In a few minutes he was back out carrying a big white box with a red bow tied around it.

"What did she get you?"

"I don't know. She said not to open it until I get home."

54

Dunc stepped on one pedal and pushed off. "Come on—I'll race you."

First Amos tried to carry the box under his arm. Then he tried to balance it on his lap. He finally had to get off and carry the box with one hand and push his bike with the other.

Dunc was waiting for him on the front porch. "What kept you?"

Amos ignored him. He dropped his bike on the lawn and headed for the front door. Dunc followed him into the living room.

Amos ripped the top off of the box. Inside was a brand-new pair of Rollerblades, a fluorescent green sweatband, and a wristband to match.

"Wow!" Amos pulled the blades out of the box. "She's *really* crazy about me!"

"Too bad you can't keep all this stuff," Dunc said.

Amos stiffened. "What do you mean?"

"I mean, you'll probably want to give it all back, considering she's out of her head and everything."

"I will?"

"Sure. It's only right. She must have

spent a lot of money on this stuff. Look at this tag. It says *Stephenson's*. That's the most expensive store in town."

Amos sighed. "I *would* have to have you around to remind me of these things. Why couldn't I have someone without a conscience for my best friend?"

Dunc shrugged. "Just lucky, I guess. Want me to help you take it back to her?"

"No. I think I'll wait awhile and figure out something better to tell her than 'I can't keep this stuff because you're nuts.'"

Dunc rubbed his chin. "You've got a point there." He snapped his fingers. "I know. We'll take the stuff back to Stephenson's ourselves. You can give the money to Melissa and tell her they didn't fit."

Amos put the blades back in the box. "You don't think maybe I should keep them? You know, on the outside chance that she really loves me?"

Dunc shook his head.

"I was afraid of that."

Chapter · 11

Stephenson's was next to the Pioneer Mall on the way toward town. Amos lived on the outskirts of town in a development. It took the boys twenty minutes to bike to the mall. It would have taken less time, but Amos was still having trouble figuring out how to carry the big white box.

Dunc locked his bike. "Want me to hold the box while you lock your bike?"

"Now he offers." Amos handed him the box. "I'll be happy to get rid of this thing. I didn't know doing the right thing was so much work."

"You'll be glad you did it when this is all

over." Dunc held the door to Stephenson's open for him.

The inside of Stephenson's looked more like an expensive hotel than a sporting goods store. The carpet was plush, and chandeliers hung from the ceiling.

A saleslady dressed like she was attending the opera headed for them. She looked Amos over for a few seconds. "May I help you, young man?"

Amos dropped the box on the counter. "Yeah. You can give me a refund for all the stuff in this box."

The woman opened the box like she expected a snake to jump out. "Do you have a receipt for this merchandise?"

Amos shook his head. "No. But everything has the name of the store right on it, so I know it came from here."

"Please wait here while I get the manager." The woman turned abruptly and walked to the back of the store. The boys could see her talking to a tall, thin man in a black suit.

"I hope this doesn't take too long." Dunc sat down on a long couch. "I need to put the finishing touches on my pretend marriage budget. It's due tomorrow."

Amos joined him on the couch. "Mrs. Wormwood said she had a bonus for the couple that did the best job. I wonder what it is?"

"I don't care, as long as I get Bertha Abercromby out of my life forever."

The man and woman walked back to the sales counter together. The man twisted his handlebar moustache. "Would you gentlemen be so kind as to tell me where you obtained this merchandise?"

Dunc stood up. "It was a gift. Is there a problem?"

"That depends. You see, this merchandise did in fact come from this store. But these things just happen to be the exact same items that were stolen from us yesterday."

"Stolen?" Amos jumped off the couch.

"I'm afraid so." The man moved around the counter. "Perhaps you could help us find the thief. Who gave these things to you?"

Chapter · 12

"There has to be some other explanation. Melissa's not a thief." Amos folded his arms and sat on Dunc's bed.

Dunc looked up from the book he was reading. "What other explanation could there be? The saleslady said she remembered a girl with long blond hair in the store yesterday. She said the girl was sweet but left without buying anything."

"So? There must be hundreds of sweet girls in this town with long blond hair. It could have been any one of them."

Dunc leaned back in his chair. "It's a good thing that salesman believed your story about finding that Rollerblade stuff wrapped in a box by your front door. Otherwise, Melissa would be in jail by now."

Amos stuck his lip out. "She didn't do it!"

A thoughtful look came over Dunc. "Amos, did you happen to notice Melissa's fingertips when you were at her house earlier?"

Amos cocked his head. "Her fingertips?"

"Yeah. They weren't black or anything, were they?"

"Now that you mention it, I did notice some black smudges on them. I thought maybe she'd been working in the garden or something." Amos sat up. "Wait a minute. You don't think Melissa is the school thief, too, do you?"

"I wonder . . ." Dunc thumbed through his book on psychiatric abnormalities. He flipped through the pages and stopped at the section on head injuries. "Hmmm. That's interesting."

"Are you going to let me in on it?"

"It says here that people who suffer head injuries often do things completely opposite from what they normally would do."

"Like ripping off expensive stores and taking things out of people's lockers?"

Dunc nodded.

Amos sank down on the bed. "What are we going to do? We can't let her go to jail."

"The book says there are only two ways to help her. The safest is to let it wear off gradually."

"What's the second way?"

Dunc turned the page. "Another bump on the head."

"Forget that. Nobody's hitting Melissa while I'm around."

"Then there's only one thing left to do."

"What?"

"You've got to return all the stuff she took and follow her everywhere she goes to make sure she doesn't take anything else."

"What do you mean, *I've* got to do it? I thought we were in on this thing together."

"I'll help when I can. But Melissa's your girlfriend. You can be around her without making her suspicious."

Amos grinned. "That has such a nice ring to it."

"What?"

"The part where you said she's my girlfriend."

"Don't get too used to it. Soon she's bound to come back to her normal self."

"But in the meantime . . ."

Dunc put the psychiatric book on his desk. "In the meantime, we have to figure out where Melissa is hiding the rest of the things she took from school and how you're going to give it all back without getting in trouble yourself."

Amos put his hands behind his head and lay back on Dunc's bed. "I'm not worried. You'll come up with something."

Chapter · 13

"And I said I wasn't worried." Amos moved a piece of shrubbery out of his nose. "In case you didn't know it, they also put you in jail for breaking and entering."

The boys were hiding in the flower garden behind Melissa's house, waiting for her mother to take her to dance class.

Dunc peeked over the hedge. "I wouldn't look at it as breaking and entering, exactly. It's more like we're a couple of uninvited guests. You know, like when your uncle Alfred comes over."

"Except everybody in my family knows when Uncle Alfred is in our house, because he takes his shoes off and picks his toes through his moldy socks. In fact I'm pretty sure even the neighbors can tell when Uncle Alfred comes to visit. It's rank."

"We won't be in there long, Amos. We'll just do a quick check and then we're out. She may not have the stuff hidden in there anyway." Dunc looked at his watch. "I thought you said Melissa was supposed to leave for dance lessons?"

The front door slammed. Melissa and her mother came rushing out and got into the station wagon.

Dunc watched from the safety of the hedge until the station wagon was well out of sight. "All clear. Let's go."

Amos tried the back door. It was locked.

"Over here." Dunc motioned for him to move to the kitchen window. "They left it open a crack. I think I can boost you up."

Amos studied the window. "I don't know —it looks pretty small."

"It's the only way in. If we go around front, somebody might spot us."

"You always have it covered, don't you? Okay, give me a boost."

Dunc pushed while Amos jumped and

grabbed the windowsill. He managed to get his head and shoulders through the tiny window, but the rest of him was stuck.

"Pull me out. I hear someone coming."

Dunc grabbed one leg and pulled. Nothing. He couldn't budge Amos. "I can't pull you out. I'm going to try pushing."

"Do something quick. Someone's coming down the stairs."

Mr. Hansen, Melissa's father, had the flu and had stayed home from work to recuperate. He went into the kitchen to get a glass of juice. He was about to open the refrigerator when he noticed Amos's head sticking through the window.

Amos tried a halfhearted smile. "Hi, Mr. Hansen. Is Melissa home?"

"*You're* one of Melissa's friends?"

Amos nodded. "Yes, sir. I'm the one she's married to."

Mr. Hansen's eyebrows came together like a black thundercloud. "What?"

"It's only pretend. Our social studies teacher gave us the assignment."

"Thank goodness. For a minute there you had me worried, son." Mr. Hansen moved closer to Amos. "Is there some reason why you're hanging through my kitchen window?"

"Yes, sir."

"Well, what is it?"

"Your back door was locked."

"I see." Mr. Hansen took the juice out of the refrigerator, scratched his head, and started back upstairs. "Must be something to do with the generation gap."

Dunc put his back against Amos's feet, braced himself against a brick flower bed, and pushed for all he was worth. Amos shot through the window and landed upside-down against the kitchen wall with his head in the cat litter box.

Dunc stood on his toes and looked through the window. "Are you all right in there?"

"*I'm* all right. But when I get the door open, *you* may not be."

Amos picked some of the cat litter out of his hair and fumbled at the lock. He was still mad when he pulled the door open. "I hope you're satisfied. Now Mr. Hansen thinks he has a complete geek for a son-in-law."

"I'm sorry, Amos. You told me to do something." Dunc sniffed the air. "What is that smell?" He sniffed closer to Amos. "It's obviously been a while since the Hansens cleaned their litter box."

Amos brushed at his hair and started out the door.

"Where are you going?" Dunc asked.

"What do you mean, where am I going? I'm going home. We can't search Melissa's room now. Her dad is here."

"So?"

Amos turned around. "We can't do it while he's in the house. He might call the cops or something."

"He won't do that. He's sick. I'll bet you anything he went upstairs to bed. We just have to be extra quiet, that's all."

Amos threw up his hands. "Why not? I think he already regrets letting Melissa marry me."

Dunc led the way up the stairs. They could hear Mr. Hansen snoring at the end of the hall. Dunc pointed to the door on the left and quietly turned the knob.

Melissa's room was decorated in pastel colors, with lace and ruffles on the curtains and bedspread. There were posters on every wall.

"Hey!" Amos was standing in front of a laminated newspaper clipping that Melissa had tacked up by her mirror.

Dunc moved over to see what Amos was looking at. It was a picture of the football team, with a red heart drawn around Biff Fastrack.

"How do you like that? My wife drew a heart around another guy's picture. What do you think it means?"

Dunc was already looking under the bed. "Everybody knows that Melissa used to like Biff before her accident."

"Rumors. Idle rumors. I don't believe a word of it."

"You're right. Next to you, how could Melissa even think about another guy—even if he is taller, stronger, and better-looking than you, not to mention captain of the football team."

"Some friend you are."

Dunc opened Melissa's closet. "Jackpot."

Melissa had a stack of notebooks and school supplies in the corner of her closet.

"Look at this." Amos picked up two white Styrofoam containers. "The lab worms." He opened the lid. "Hey Rover, Rex—easy, guys! I'm here. It's all right."

Dunc stared at him for a moment, then shrugged and started gathering up the notebooks. "Help me carry this stuff. We have to be out of here before Melissa gets home."

"She must have hit every locker in school," Amos said. "What are we going to do with it?"

"We'll worry about that later. For now, let's get going."

Dunc made his way carefully down the stairs. Amos followed, carrying a stack of items taller than his head. The two Styrofoam containers were balanced on top.

Just as Dunc reached for the door, it was yanked open, and Mrs. Hansen bustled in. "I forgot my—Oh, dear." She tried to get a look at the boys' faces around the school supplies. "Do I know you people?"

Mr. Hansen had come back downstairs for another glass of juice. He walked past the boys as if they weren't there. "Don't worry, dear. They're Melissa's friends. She's married to the one with the cap." He filled his glass and headed back upstairs.

Mrs. Hansen hesitated and then hurried after him. "Wait, Edward. No one told me Melissa was married. Why am I always the last to know these things?"

Amos looked at Dunc around the edge of his stack. "And I thought my parents were strange."

Chapter · 14

Amos was dreaming. It was visiting day in the big house. Jail. He passed through several heavy iron gates, which clanged shut behind him. The inmates were reaching for him through the bars and calling him Hunk-Ra.

Finally, he made it to the visiting room. Melissa was waiting for him. Only she wasn't the same girl he remembered. Her hair was dirty and stringy, and she was wearing a striped suit. Amos looked down and saw a heavy ball and chain attached to her ankle. She was smoking a smelly cigar and kept saying "You dirty rat."

"Amos, wake up." Dunc shook him. Amos

didn't open his eyes. Dunc got down on his knees and yelled next to Amos's ear, *"Wake up!"* Amos opened one eye and muttered something about the possibility of parole in twenty years. Then he closed it again and pulled the cover over his head.

Dunc shrugged. "Only one thing left to do." He went to the hall and whistled.

In less than a minute, Scruff, the Binder family dog, came running. Actually, Scruff was not the entire Binder family's dog. He hated one particular member of the family: Amos. Years ago, the collie had put Amos on his hit list. Dunc never knew the exact reason—it had something to do with Amos and a hot burrito.

Scruff, being the vengeful dog he was, grabbed the corner of the bedspread and pulled it off the bed. Then he backed up to the door like a bull ready to charge, exploded full speed toward the bed, and jumped. He landed like a ton of bricks in the middle of Amos's stomach.

"Aaagggh!" Amos curled into a ball. When he got his wind back, he sat up and glared at the dog. Scruff sat on the edge of the bed and wagged his tail.

74

"Okay, boy. That'll do." Dunc patted his head.

"Don't pat that mutt," Amos said. "He's nothing but a flea-bitten waste of space."

Scruff dived at Amos's feet. He came up with a big toe.

"Let go of me, you stupid mongrel."

Dunc coaxed and called, but Scruff wouldn't let go. Dunc scratched his head. "I think he wants you to say you're sorry."

"Okay. I'm sorry already."

Scruff let go and trotted out of the room.

Amos threw a pillow after him. "Dumb dog. One of these days, I'm taking him on a tour of the city pound and only one of us is coming back."

Dunc smiled. "I wouldn't want to take bets on which one."

"Very funny." Amos scowled and looked at his alarm clock. "Do you realize it's five o'clock? In the morning?"

"We have a lot to do today, remember?"

"No." Amos yawned and started to lie back down.

"Let me see if I can jog your memory. It has to do with keeping a certain girl we know out of major trouble."

Amos sat up. "Melissa!" He reached for his pants, which were right where he had taken them off the night before—on the floor.

Dunc went out to the hall and brought in a cardboard box. "We'll sneak everything she took into the school lost-and-found department before anybody gets there this morning. And then you'll still have time to make it back to Melissa's house to walk her to school. Don't forget, you can't let her out of your sight. You have to walk her to every class and stay with her every minute between classes."

Amos still had his pajama shirt on. He tucked it in, pulled a cap down over his uncombed hair, and headed for the door. "Not a problem."

Chapter · **15**

Amos fell into an exhausted heap onto the bench in the cafeteria. "I'm beat," he told Dunc. "You wouldn't believe what I've been through today. Not only did I have to run all the way to Melissa's house this morning, I had to rush her to class and then try to get to mine before the bell. After class, I had to hustle to keep her from leaving without me."

Dunc took a bite of his sandwich. "Why aren't you with her now?"

"She's eating lunch with some girls. She'll be okay." He wiped the perspiration off his forehead. "I didn't realize having Melissa for a girlfriend would be so much work."

"This afternoon should be a little easier for you. Mrs. Wormwood is letting our class go to the gym to decorate for parents' night."

"We're having a parents' night? When?"

"Amos, don't you ever pay attention? The principal made the announcement last week."

"I must have missed it. Is this going to be one of those things where your parents go around and visit your teachers and ask them what kind of grades you're making?"

Dunc nodded.

"As if I don't have enough problems." Amos reached over and grabbed one of Dunc's cookies. "Maybe I'll accidentally forget to tell them about it."

"No good. The school is sending out invitations."

Amos shrugged. "Well, I guess I'll just have to bring my grades up between now and then."

Dunc looked at him. "In two days?"

"Maybe you can help me do some extra-credit reports or something."

Dunc was about to explain to Amos that even if they had enough time to write the reports, the teachers wouldn't have time to grade them in two days. But he was cut short because the bell rang and Melissa headed through the cafeteria door by herself.

Amos jumped up. "Catch you later, Dunc. Duty calls."

Chapter · 16

"Some bonus." Dunc sat in the corner of the gym on a pile of tumbling mats. "I thought hard work was supposed to pay off—you know, get you someplace in life."

"Don't let it get to you," Amos said. "Your marriage budget made the best grade in class."

"Yeah, and look what it got me. Host of parents' night, with Bertha Abercromby as hostess. We have to sit together all night."

Amos was trying to console his friend and keep an eye on Melissa at the same time. "Uh-oh. She's at it again."

Dunc looked up. Melissa was following Brittany Wilkes. As soon as Brittany put up a decoration, Melissa would take it down and stuff it into her book bag.

Amos raced over to Melissa. "Hi, honeybunch. You're sure doing a good job decorating the gym and everything. Maybe I could help."

Amos reached into her book bag and started putting the decorations back up. He motioned for Dunc to come and help.

Melissa pulled on the bag. "That's okay, cupcake. I can manage."

Mrs. Wormwood was looking in their direction.

Dunc helped Amos pull on the bag. They almost had it when Mrs. Wormwood walked over. "What's going on here?"

The boys let go of the bag. The only problem was that Melissa still had a good grip. She fell backward. She might have been okay if Herman Snodgrass hadn't been on his hands and knees painting a "Welcome, Parents" sign right behind her.

She flipped over Herman, knocked over the can of paint, and landed in the bleachers.

Amos ran to her. She was out cold. He

fanned her and tried slapping her hand. "Sweet-face, speak to me!"

By now, the whole class had moved to the bleachers and was watching. Mrs. Wormwood had gone for the nurse.

Amos looked at Dunc. "Maybe I better try mouth-to-mouth."

"It wouldn't help. You only use that if they're not breathing."

"I know."

Melissa opened her eyes. She looked up at Amos. "Where am I?"

"In the gym. Don't worry, pumpkin, I'm here with you."

Melissa stared at him. "Who are you?" She pushed him out of her way and sat up. "What am I doing here? Where's Biff?" She stood up and headed for the gym door.

Amos ran after her. "Wait, snookems! Don't you remember? We balanced our checkbooks together!"

Dunc watched them go and shook his head. "Well, at least things are back to normal."

He looked over and saw Tall Bertha waving at him. He hid his face with his jacket. "Wait, Amos! I'll trade you two extra-credit reports if you'll be host on parents' night.

"Amos!"

The Culpepper Cupid Quiz
by Amos Binder, The Love God

Test your romantic know-how by answering the following questions written by Amos, The Love God. Proceed, if you dare.

1. You know you are in love when . . .
    a. you actually *want* to go to school.
    b. you wake up before your alarm goes off and get up early so you can follow your love when she walks to school.
    c. you wear deodorant.
    d. None of the above.
2. If your love doesn't seem to know you exist, you should . . .
    a. pretend *she* doesn't exist (it's reverse psychology).
    b. send her love letters, unsigned.
    c. follow her around until she's scared of you.
    d. None of the above.

3. You know she's starting to like you when she . . .
   a. doesn't kick you as hard as she used to.
   b. smiles at someone you've met.
   c. looks in your direction when you scream out her name.
   d. None of the above.
4. The best way to spark her interest is to . . .
   a. tell her the one about the pig with a scab.
   b. pick a fight with the class bully— the big kid who's been held back four grades.
   c. tell nasty stories about the school principal in front of her.
   d. None of the above.
5. You can tell it's not working if . . .
   a. she won't sign the body cast you've worn since you took on the class bully.
   b. she turns you in to the principal for the things you said.
   c. now, instead of kicking you, she pays the class bully to do it.
   d. None of the above.
6. The absolute most romantic thing you can think of doing for a girl is to . . .
   a. give her a dozen carp.

b. stand outside her window at night and sing all the verses to "Ninety-nine Bottles of Beer on the Wall."

c. buy her four pounds of unsweetened baking chocolate for her birthday.

d. None of the above.

7. You can tell how much she likes *you* by . . .

a. how hard her friends laugh at you when you walk by. (They're happy for you.)

b. how often the phone rings when you're near.

c. how insistently she ignores you. (She's playing hard to get.)

d. None of the above.

8. For your first date you should . . .

a. teach her how to spit.

b. ask her to help you clean your room.

c. take her to see the World Wrestling Federation battle of the bellies.

d. None of the above.

9. When dining with your date you should . . .

a. use your sleeve instead of your napkin. (It shows you are conservation-minded.)

b. use your tongue to lick your plate. (All girls respect a healthy appetite.)

c. impress her by eating spaghetti through your nose. (It works with the guys in the cafeteria.)

d. None of the above.

10. When you meet her parents you should . . .

   a. tell them the one about the cow with a scab.

   b. tell her father about your future as a professional stunt man.

   c. ask them how they managed to have such a beautiful daughter, being as ugly as they are.

   d. None of the above.

Scoring Your Official Cupid Quiz:
by Dunc Culpepper, The Voice of Reason

Give yourself one point for each time you *didn't* answer "d. None of the above." Then rate yourself against Dunc's scale:

Total Points:	Dunc's clearance to date:
1 (or less)	Hope you've got an after-school job. You could be married within the week.
2 or 3	Look forward to a few hot dates.
4 or 5	You have clearance, provided you wear deodorant and don't eat baked beans the night before.
6	Strong chance she may turn you down and go out with your best friend.
7	She'll probably say no and become a nun because boys

scare her now, but at least she knows you exist.

8 . . . . Maybe you should consider becoming a nun yourself.

9 . . . . The only reason your mom is seen with you is because they throw negligent parents in jail.

10 . . . . Give it up. The only person who cares about you is your dog, and he growls when you're around.

271 . . . . Amos's score. (He took the quiz more than once.)

Be sure to join Dunc and Amos in these other Culpepper Adventures:

The Case of the Dirty Bird

When Dunc Culpepper and his best friend, Amos, first see the parrot in a pet store, they're not impressed—it's smelly, scruffy, and missing half its feathers. They're only slightly impressed when they learn that the parrot speaks four languages, has outlived ten of its owners, and is probably 150 years old. But when the bird starts mouthing off about buried treasure, Dunc and Amos get pretty excited—let the amateur sleuthing begin!

Dunc's Doll

Dunc and his accident-prone friend Amos are up to their old sleuthing habits once again. This time they're after a band of doll thieves! When a doll that once belonged to Charles Dickens's daughter is stolen from an exhibition at the local mall, the two boys put on their detective gear and do some serious snooping. Will a vicious watch dog keep them from retrieving the valuable missing doll?

Culpepper's Cannon

Dunc and Amos are researching the Civil War cannon that stands in the town square when they find a note inside telling them about a time portal. Entering it through the dressing room of La Petite, a women's clothing store, the boys find themselves in downtown Chatham on March 8, 1862—the day before the historic clash between the *Monitor* and the *Merrimac*. But the Confederate soldiers they meet mistake them for Yankee spies. Will they make it back to the future in one piece?

Dunc Gets Tweaked

Dunc and Amos meet up with a new buddy named Lash when they enter the radical world of skateboard competition. When somebody "cops"—steals—Lash's prototype skateboard, the boys are determined to get it back. After all, Lash is about to shoot for a totally rad world's record! Along the way they learn a major lesson: *Never* kiss a monkey!

Dunc's Halloween

Dunc and Amos are planning the best route to get the most candy on Halloween. But their plans change when Amos is slightly bitten by a werewolf. He begins scratching himself and chasing UPS trucks—he's become a werepuppy!

Dunc Breaks the Record

Dunc and Amos have a small problem when they try hang gliding—they crash in the wilderness. Luckily, Amos has read a book about a boy who survived in the wilderness for fifty-four days. Too bad Amos doesn't have a hatchet. Things go from bad to worse when a wild man holds the boys captive. Can anything save them now?

Dunc and the Flaming Ghost

Dunc's not afraid of ghosts, although Amos is sure that the old Rambridge house is haunted by the ghost of Blackbeard the Pirate. Then the best friends meet Eddie, a meek man who claims to be impersonating Blackbeard's ghost in order to live in the house in peace. But if that's true, why are flames shooting from his mouth?

Amos Gets Famous

Deciphering a code they find in a library book, Amos and Dunc stumble onto a burglary ring. The burglars' next target is the home of Melissa, the girl of Amos's dreams (who doesn't even know that he's alive). Amos longs to be a hero to Melissa, so nothing will stop him from solving this case—not even a mind-boggling collision with a jock, a chimpanzee, and a toilet.

Dunc and Amos Hit the Big Top

In order to impress Melissa, Amos decides to perform on the trapeze at the visiting circus. Look out below! But before Dunc can talk him out of his plan, the two stumble across a mystery behind the scenes at the circus. Now Amos is in double trouble. What's really going on under the big top?

Dunc's Dump

Camouflaged as piles of rotting trash, Dunc and Amos are sneaking around the town dump. Dunc wants to find out who is polluting the garbage at the dump with hazardous and toxic waste. Amos just wants to impress Melissa. Can either of them succeed?

Dunc and the Scam Artists

Dunc and Amos are at it again. Some older residents of their town have been bilked by con artists, and the two boys want to look into these crimes. They meet elderly Betsy Dell, whose nasty nephew Frank gives the boys the creeps. Then they notice some soft dirt in Ms. Dell's shed, and a shovel. Does Frank have something horrible in store for Dunc and Amos?

Dunc and Amos and the Red Tattoos

Dunc and Amos head for camp and face two weeks of fresh air—along with regulations, demerits, KP, and inedible food. But where these two best friends go, trouble follows. They overhear a threat against the camp director, and discover that camp funds have been stolen. Do these crimes have anything to do with the tattoo of the exotic red flower that some of the camp staff have on their arms?

Dunc's Undercover Christmas

It's Christmastime, and Dunc, Amos, and Amos's cousin T.J. hit the mall for some serious shopping. But when the seasonal magic is threatened by some disappearing presents, and Santa Claus himself is a prime suspect, the boys put their celebration on hold and go undercover in perfect Christmas disguises! Can the sleuthing trio protect Santa's threatened reputation and catch the impostor before he strikes again?

The Wild Culpepper Cruise

When Amos wins a "Why I Love My Dog" contest, he and Dunc are off on the Caribbean cruise of their dreams! But there's something downright fishy about Amos's suitcase, and before they know it, the two best friends wind up with more high-seas adventure than they bargained for. Can Dunc and Amos figure out who's out to get them and salvage what's left of their vacation?

Dunc and the Haunted Castle

When Dunc and Amos are invited to spend a week in Scotland, Dunc can already hear the bagpipes a-blowin'. But when the boys spend their first night in an ancient castle, it isn't bagpipes they hear. It's moans! Dunc hears groaning coming from inside his bedroom walls. Amos notices the eyes of a painting follow him across the room! Could the castle really be haunted? Local legend has it that the castle's former lord wanders the ramparts at night in search of his head! Team up with Dunc and Amos as they go ghostbusting in the Scottish Highlands!

Cowpokes and Desperadoes

Git along, little dogies! Dunc and Amos are bound for Uncle Woody Culpepper's Santa Fe cattle ranch for a week of fun. But when they overhear a couple of cowpokes plotting to do Uncle Woody in, the two sleuths are back on the trail of some serious action! Who's been making off with all the prize cattle? Can Dunc and Amos stop the rustlers in time to save the ranch?

Prince Amos

When their fifth-grade class spends a weekend interning at the state capital, Dunc and Amos find themselves face-to-face with Amos's walking double—Prince Gustav, Crown Prince of Moldavia! His Royal Highness is desperate to uncover a traitor in his ranks. And when he asks Amos to switch places with him, Dunc holds his breath to see what will happen next. Can Amos pull off the impersonation of a lifetime?

Coach Amos

Amos and Dunc have their hands full when their school principal asks *them* to coach a local T-ball team. For one thing, nobody on the team even knows first base from left field, and the season opener is coming right up. And then there's that sinister-looking gangster driving by in his long black limo and making threats. Can Dunc and Amos fend off screaming tots, nervous mothers, and the mob, and be there when the ump yells "Play ball"?

Amos and the Alien

When Amos and his best friend Dunc have a close encounter with an extraterrestrial named Girrk, Dunc thinks they should report their findings to NASA. But Amos has other plans. He not only promises to help Girrk find a way back to his planet, he invites him to hide out under his bed! Then weird things start to happen—Scruff can't move, Amos scores a game-winning *touchdown,* and Dunc knows Girrk is behind Amos's new powers. What's the mysterious alien really up to?

Dunc and Amos Meet the Slasher

Why is mild-mannered Amos dressed in leather, slicking back his hair, strutting around the cafeteria, and going by a phony name? Could it be because of that new kid, Slasher, who's promised to eat Amos for lunch? Or has Amos secretly gone undercover? Amos and his pal Dunc have some hot leads and are close to cracking a stolen stereo racket, but Dunc is worried Amos has taken things too far!

Dunc and the Greased Sticks of Doom

Five . . . four . . . three . . . two . . . Olympic superstar Francesco Bartoli is about to hurl himself down the face of a mountain in another attempt to clinch the world slalom speed record. Cheering fans and snapping cameras are everywhere. But someone is out to stop him, and Dunc thinks he knows who it is. Can Dunc get to the gate in time to save the day? Will Amos survive longer than fifteen minutes on the icy slopes?

Join best friends Dunc Culpepper and Amos Binder as they take an action-packed winter ski vacation filled with fun, fame, and high-speed high jinx.

Amos's Killer Concert Caper

Amos is desperate. He's desperate for two tickets to the romantic event of his young life . . . the Road Kill concert! He'll do anything to get them because he heard from a friend of a friend of a friend of Melissa Hansen that she's way into Road Kill. But when he enlists the help of his best friend Dunc, he winds up with more than he bargained for . . . backstage, with a mystery to solve. Somebody's trying to make Road Kill live up to their name. Can Dunc and Amos find out who and keep the music playing?

For laugh-out-loud fun, join Dunc and Amos and take the Culpepper challenge!
Gary Paulsen's Culpepper Adventures—
Bet you can't read just one!

☐ 0-440-40790-7 DUNC AND AMOS AND THE RED TATTOOS.....$3.25/$3.99 Can.

☐ 0-440-40874-1 DUNC'S UNDERCOVER CHRISTMAS...............$3.50/$4.50 Can.

☐ 0-440-40883-0 THE WILD CULPEPPER CRUISE......................$3.50/$4.50 Can.

☐ 0-440-40893-8 DUNC AND THE HAUNTED CASTLE.................$3.50/$4.50 Can.

☐ 0-440-40902-0 COWPOKES AND DESPERADOES....................$3.50/$4.50 Can.

☐ 0-440-40928-4 PRINCE AMOS..$3.50/$4.50 Can.

☐ 0-440-40930-6 COACH AMOS...$3.50/$4.50 Can.

☐ 0-440-40990-X AMOS AND THE ALIENS...................................$3.50/$4.50 Can.

Bantam Doubleday Dell
Books for Young Readers

Bantam Doubleday Dell Books for Young Readers
2451 South Wolf Road
Des Plaines, IL 60018

Please send the items I have checked above. I'm enclosing $_____ (please add $2.50 to cover postage and handling). Send check or money order, no cash or C.O.D.s please.

Name _____

Address _____

City _____ State _____ Zip _____

Please allow four to six weeks for delivery.
Prices and availability subject to change without notice.   BFYR 29 6/94

Check Out This All-Star Lineup From Sports Illustrated For Kids®!

There's no cooler place to find jammin' books about your favorite athletes! **Sports Illustrated For Kids®** has got it all—from biographies about your favorite sports stars to brain-teasing puzzle books to a sports encyclopedia that puts the world of sports at your fingertips.

Order any or all of these exciting selections. Just check out our lineup, check off the titles you want, then fill out and mail the order form below!